T0209769

FARM BRIDGE

Station Series

Peter's Day

Balboa Press books may be ordered through booksellers or by contacting:

Balboa Press
A Division of Hay House
1663 Liberty Drive
Bloomington, IN 47403
www.balboapress.com.au
1 (877) 407-4847

ISBN: 978-1-5043-1749-8 (sc)
ISBN: 978-1-5043-1750-4 (e)

Interior Graphics/Art Credit: Gareth Pennington

Print information available on the last page.

Balboa Press rev. date: 04/09/2019

BALBOA
PRESS
A DIVISION OF HAY HOUSE

Peter's Day

To:_____

_____

Written and illustrated by: Gareth Pennington
Editor: Laureen Newsham
Published by Balboa Publications
© Copyright 2018

FARM BRIDGE
Station Series

A gentle summer breeze blew through the window across Peter sleeping peacefully.

Outside the birds tweeted, chattered and flitted around in the red gum trees, announcing the sun as it peeked over the tree tops.

Ding, Ding, Ding, Ding!

"Ahhhhh!" shouted Peter, woken by his bedside alarm clock.
"Paul!" he exclaimed, annoyed that his brother had set the clock to wake him up and it wasn't even a school day!

Peter stretched his arms and looked out his bedroom window.
"Yesssss!" he said to himself quietly as he looked out across his yard and into the paddocks. Paddocks that were covered in sheep with the odd kangaroo here and there. This day was beautifully soaked in blue sky and sunshine, a great day to spend outdoors exploring.

Bang! The door swung open and in bounded Blue. In sheer excitement the cattle dog jumped straight on to the bed, on top of Peter who screamed out with laughter as Blue gave him a morning bath, right across his face.

"Ahhh Blue! Stop it," Peter said, in between laughing and wiping away Blue's slobber.

"Okay, enough of that, Blue. Off the bed," said Peter's dad sternly.
"Okey Dokey, Peter. Time to get out of bed and get going. We have a bit to do this morning......and I set the alarm clock, not Paul."

"Yep, Dad did," said Paul, as he stood in the doorway with a big grin on his face.

"No need to chase Mum for breakfast," said Peter's dad. "We have what we need here in my tucker bag. Get dressed quickly and meet us downstairs by the truck."

"But it's Saturday," whined Peter.

"I'll have none of that now, young man. We spoke about this last night at the dinner table," said Peter's dad. "Come on now, it's time to get moving. The sooner we start, the sooner we finish and then you boys can go off to the Stephenson's station and spend time with your mates. Besides, we're only checking the cattle's water troughs in the back paddock."

"The back paddock! That paddock is 10 kilometers away and they probably need cleaning too," complained Peter. "Yuuuck," he mumbled, as he took more time to get dressed.

"What's that, son?"

"Nothing, Dad. Just talking to Blue."

Blue looked up at Peter with a puzzled look on his face.
(*If any dog could have a puzzled look, it would be Blue. Head tilted sideways, eyes wide open and ears pointing straight up.*)

"Come on, Blue!" shouted Peter as they both raced through the upstairs hall and down the stairs, nearly tripping over each other as they ran out the back door at the same time. **Slam!**

"Peter!" shouted Annie, Peter's mum.

"Sorry, Mum!" replied Peter.

"Morning Mum? Bye Mum? Don't I get a hug anymore?" asked Peter's mum with one hand placed firmly on her hip.

Peter turned around sharply and raced back to hug his mother.

"Morning, Mum," he said softly as he wrapped his arms around her waist, giving her a great big squeeze. "I'll see you later, Mum. Okay?" he said with raised eyebrows and a rather convincing nod. "Oh......and I'm going to Tom's after we finish working with Dad."

"I know, Peter. Don't be late for dinner."

"Yes, Mum."

"Don't go getting into any trouble......and don't you boys go catching snakes again!" said Annie with a raised, stern voice as she pointed her telling off finger towards him.

"Yes, Mum."

"After all, you remember what happened last time."

"Yes, Mum! I got ta go!" as he started to hop up and down with some impatience.

"Annie, let the boy go," said Dave.

"Okay, off you go then and have a good morning, boys," said Annie.

"See ya!" said Alice as she popped her head around Mum's leg.

Alice, Peter's little sister, is a pint-sized bundle, with long blonde hair, big blue eyes, and rosy red cheeks. She was wearing her favorite sunflower covered dress and holding her best friend, Ted the bear.

"See ya, Alice," said Peter as he stooped down to kiss the top of her head.

"Come on, Peter! The day's not getting any younger," said Dad.

"Coming, Dad!" replied Peter. "Ahh, Henry!" yelled Peter as he ran to the truck, nearly tripping over the old tom cat who had come out to have a look at what all the fuss was about.

"Get in the back with Blue, son. There's not enough room up front for all three of us," said Dad.

Peter jumped in the back with Blue. "Not much room in the back either with all the work tools!" thought Peter.

"Peter, make sure Blue's tied up in the middle of the tray. We don't want him falling out or jumping off to chase rabbits again," said Dad.

"Yep, will do, Dad," said Peter.

Off they went in the old, beat up 4 wheel drive tray top that had seen better days. Paul calls it the 'old boneshaker'. Annie calls it 'the old money pit'. Dave......well he says, "Best work mate I've ever had. Never let me down. Still does the job. Keeps on going and I can fix it myself. Ain't changing a thing."

"Things are looking a bit dry out here. Hope the windmills have been pumping water," said Dave.

"Daaaad!" shouted Paul, pointing out the front of the truck. Dave was busy looking out his side window at the dry undergrowth in the Mallee scrub.

Dave slammed on the brakes, the truck shuddered, shook and bounced to a stop, dust and dirt flying everywhere. Peter, Blue, and all the tools slid into each other and into the back of the truck cabin.

"Oww!" Peter shouted. Blue yelped at first and then started barking, trying to get out of the truck.

"Dad, what's going on? **Blue!**" yelled Peter, trying to get his attention and stop him from barking.

"What's going on, Dad?" shouted Peter again with a rather worried look on his face.

"Snake on the road!" came the shout from the driver's seat.

So there they were, all four of them, gazing out through the front window of the truck with stunned looks on their faces at what they were seeing before them.

Blue was the first to break the silence, barking boldly, tail wagging frantically in the air.

"Look at the size of that!" said Peter, with both eyebrows raised, pointing excitedly at the massive scrub python.

"That's the biggest I have ever seen," said Paul, as he turned to look at his dad.

"**Blue! stop that barking!**" Dave shouted. "Peter, will ya see to that dog?"

"Yep that's the biggest sucker I have ever seen," said Dave. "And it looks like it's just had lunch. Look at that bulge in it!"

"Looks like it ate a 'roo," said Paul.

"Nah, 'roos are too big to eat. It'll be a joey or a wallaby. Rock Wallaby most likely. There's a mob of them that live in those rocky hills over there," said Dad.

"Awesome!" said Peter. "It's bigger than the truck! Can I get a closer look Dad?"

"No way mister! You just stay in the back and let it go by. You can see it well enough from back there."

"Wish Tom was here to see this. Wish I had a camera with me, too. He's never going to believe how big it is!" said Peter.

"Okay, let's get moving," said Dad.

After 20 minutes of bone-rattling ruts, dips, a snake and a river crossing, they arrived at the first water trough.

"Okay, boys. Let's get to work. We've got three more to check after this one."

"Well, this one looks good," Dave mumbled to himself, as he leaned over and looked inside.

"Paul, you check the windmill. It's pumping water okay but there's a squeak in the gears. I can hear it from here. Paul, take the grease and small tool bag with you. Oh.....and don't forget to turn the gears off and lock the blades."

"Okay, Dad. Leave it to me," said Paul.

"Peter, you and I will check out the trough and clean it if needed and go let Blue off the chain so he can run and stretch his legs," said Dad.

Blue couldn't contain his excitement as Peter let him loose. He tore around and around them in big circles as they tried to work, kicking up small clouds of dust with his paws.

"I must say, good work boys. This one's done already. On to the next one now," said their dad. "I hope all are the same today."

After the third trough was done, Dave wiped his dusty hands on his jeans, feeling rather pleased with their progress.

"Well, we're onto the last one now boys," said Dave. "It's looking like we might be finished earlier than I thought."

"Yessss," said Peter to himself. "The earlier the better. More time for playing with my best friend."

"All in the truck. Let's get to the fourth one. Peter, get Blue," said Peter's dad.

The fourth water trough was further out into the mallee scrub.

Paul spotted a few feral pigs on the way and pointed them out to his dad.

"They are one of the biggest pests out here," Dad explained. "They do a lot of damage to the water holes and troughs and also to the native scrub and animals. They even took one of the Stevenson's calves last week and injured two others. Those razorback pigs can be pretty nasty."

Talking about pigs had caused time to go fast in the truck and before they knew it, they were already at the last waterhole for the day.

"Ewww! It's full of algae and mud," said Peter, screwing up his nose. "Looks like there's a leak. There is a lot of mud and churned up ground on the other side."

"Hmmm, this does not look good," said Dave with concern. "Not good at all," he said with a frown on his face. "Wild pigs have been using it." Dave pointed to the ground. "Look boys? You can see their tracks and where they have been wallowing in the mud."

"Yep, I see," said Peter. "There's quite a few of them. Different sized tracks too."

"You haven't let Blue off the chain yet have you?" Dave asked Peter.

"No, Dad. He's still in the tray," answered Peter.

"Good, don't let him off here. We don't need him stirring things up if pigs are around. Now, I want you both to keep your eyes open and your wits about you," said Dave.

"Yes, Dad," Peter and Paul answered as they glanced sideways at each other.

"Now let's get cracking, hey boys," said Dad. "Same as the other three: Paul to the windmill, Peter and I will attend to the water trough."

Paul sprinted across to the windmill as Peter and Dave walked back to the truck to get the tools, Blue kicked up an almighty fuss, barking, growling, straining against the chain, trying to break free.

"Piiiiiig!" Paul screamed from on top of the windmill, **"Watch out!** Razorback! Behind you!"

Dave turned first. There it was. A massive, dirty, muddy, fly-riddled, large tusked, black, grunting pig coming around the right side of the water trough. It had a large scar from its snout to forehead.

"Nooo," he said to himself. When Dave saw the scar on the pig's face, he remembered what his mate, John Stephenson, had told him just two weeks before. A pig had taken one of his calves and mauled two others. John had described the pig in detail, with a particular comment about the scar that streched from snout to forehead.

'Feral pigs will eat anything and will attack anything that moves or runs,' John had told him. That's what had stuck in Dave's mind the most.

"Peter! don't move," Dad murmured in a low voice so as not to startle the pig.

But Peter had already started to turn around to see where the pig was.

"Peter, whatever you do, stand still!
Don't move!" his dad shouted, but as
Peter was turning around, he tripped and
fell head first into cow patties and mud.

"Aaaaaghh yuck!" said Peter. **"Daaaaad!"** he screamed, realising with terror what danger he was in.

At this the pig, which had been intently focused on Blue making all the noise and didn't see Peter at first, started trotting towards the boy.

Dave raced to the truck, grabbed his rifle from the back window sill and ran hurriedly back trying to steady himself to get a clear shot.

BANG! "Ahhhh, no, no, no!" Dave missed!

"Dad! Hurry up!" screamed Paul from on top of the windmill, anxiously jumping up and down.

Blue, barking and growling and showing all his teeth, pulled so hard that he finally broke the chain and headed straight for the pig. The pig was four times bigger than him but that did not matter to Blue. His best mate was in trouble.

Peter was frozen in mud and cow poop. He screamed. The last thing he saw was the Razorback running straight towards him before squeezing his eyes tightly shut.

BANG!

Everything went deadly quiet. Paul stood motionless on top of the windmill. Blue stopped running. Dave with feet anchored to the ground just stood looking desperately at Peter who was frozen in fright.

"Peter! Peter!" Dad shouted out as his feet unlocked and he started moving towards his son but Peter still didn't move. When Dave heard a noise coming from the scrub he spun round, frantic to see what or who it was.

"Peter!" called out a little voice from a distance. It was Tom, Peter's mate, with his dad, John. Tom's dad was holding a smoking rifle, the rifle that had just stopped the razorback in its tracks.

To Dave's great relief, Peter began to finally stir, slowly opening his eyes to look straight into the eyes of the dead, hairy, extremely smelly pig. Peter could see the dirt-encrusted wrinkles of skin, hair, yellow stained tusks and the scar that stretched from snout to forehead.

Tom walked up to Peter and the pig. "I don't think I know who looks and smells the worst. You or the pig?" he said with a big grin on his face.

"Not funny, Tom," snapped Peter.

"Ha, Ha, Ha!" Tom couldn't help himself from laughing. "Yep, it's you alright. The pig looks better," said Tom as he helped pick Peter up.

"You alright, son?" asked Dave.

"Yes, Dad," said Peter.

By then John and Paul had made their way over to Peter as well.

"Thanks, mate," said Dave to John as he reached out to shake his hand. "I owe you big time. I don't know what we would have done if you were not around."

"That's ok, mate. Glad I was. Been tracking Ol' Scar since early morning. He took another of my calves last night."

"You all good, Peter?" asked John as he patted the top of Peter's head.

"Yes, Uncle John, I'm alright."

Peter turned around and Tom cracked up laughing again. He was in absolute stitches. John could see what his son Tom was laughing at and couldn't help himself. He burst into laughter too. Even Dave and his brother, Paul, finally gave in and laughed.

Peter was not amused."Hey! What are you all laughing at anyway? It's not at all funny. I could have been badly hurt!" Peter said angrily. Then Blue started to bark, looking up at him with his big brown eyes.

"Aw, not you too," said Peter putting his hands on his hips.

Peter stormed off to the truck and as he walked past the side view mirror he caught a glance of his face. He stopped and stared at himself and then burst out into outrageous, belly-jiggling laughter at the sight. Stuck to his face was a wet, sloppy, green cow pat and all he could see was his mouth, nose and eyes poking through.

"Alright, alright," said Dave. "Let's clean up now and get on our way. It is getting late." "John, you and Tom can get a ride with us if you like. After all, that's the least I can do."

"All good, Dave. You would've done the same for me," said John.

"So, do you still want this smelly, muddy boy at your place?" Dave asked John cheekily.

"Yep," he nodded. "That'll be okay with me. He can even stay the night if he wants to. Tom would love the company. Peter can have some of Tom's clothes to wear and to save you coming back to pick him up, we can drop Peter off on the way to church tomorrow morning if you like?"

"Yesss!" said Tom happily. "Can he, Uncle Dave?"

"Can I please, Dad?" asked Peter.

"Okay, okay, you can," said Dave with a smile. "I'll just have to give Annie a call from your house if that's ok John, to let her know what's going on. Oh and hey, nothing about the pig. Okay? I'll let her know when I get home."

Finishing up they piled into the truck, John and Dave in front, boys in the back tray with Blue.

"Hey, Peter. Glad you're okay," said Tom.

"Me too," said Paul.

"Hey Tom, I nearly forgot to tell you. You should have seen this big scrub python we nearly ran over today! **It was this big!**" Peter said, streching his arms out." Of course, the snake grew in size as Peter told the story.

"Really? No way!" gasped Tom. "Hey, guess what. We found a cave on the way while chasing that pig," said Tom to Peter.

"No way! How large?" asked Peter.

"Don't know. We didn't go in. Maybe we can ask my dad to take us there tomorrow and go check it out. If we are allowed," said Tom.

"What a day!" They all said at the same time. Looked at one another with surprised expressions on their faces, everyone burst out laughing as the truck went shaking, rattling and bouncing back down the track.

You could just faintly hear John tell Dave..........."You need a new truck, mate."

**LOOK OUT FOR THE NEXT BOOK
IN THE FARMBRIDGE STATION SERIES
AS OUR FAVORITE CHARACTERS
PETER, TOM & PAUL GO EXPLORING**

FARMBRIDGE Station Series

The Cave

Written and illustrated by: Gareth Pennington
Editor: Laureen Newsham
Published by Balboa Publications
© Copyright 2018

Printed in the United States
By Bookmasters